MOUSE'S FIRST CHRISTMAS

Lauren Thompson

ILLUSTRATED BY

Buket Erdogan

SCHOLASTIC INC.

New York Toronto London Auckland Sydney
Mexico City New Delhi Hong Kong

To Kevin ❖ L.T.

To Mom, Dad, and my husband, Yucel ❖ B.E.

No part of this publication may be reproduced in whole or in part, or stored
in a retrieval system, or transmitted in any form or by any means, electronic,
mechanical, photocopying, recording, or otherwise, without written permission
of the publisher. For information regarding permission, write to Simon &
Schuster Books for Young Readers, an imprint of Simon & Schuster Children's
Publishing Division, 1230 Avenue of the Americas, New York, NY 10020.

ISBN 0-439-21879-9

Text copyright © 1999 by Lauren Thompson. Illustrations copyright © 1999 by
Buket Erdogan. All rights reserved. Published by Scholastic Inc.,
555 Broadway, New York, NY 10012, by arrangement with Simon & Schuster
Books for Young Readers, an imprint of Simon & Schuster Children's Publishing
Division. SCHOLASTIC and associated logos are trademarks and/or registered
trademarks of Scholastic Inc.

12 11 10 9 8 7 6 5 4 3 2 1   1 2 3 4 5/0

Printed in the U.S.A.   14

First Scholastic printing, November 2000
Book design by Heather Wood

'Twas a night still and starry
and all through the house,
not a creature was stirring...

just one little mouse.

Mouse was peeking all around
to see what good things
could be found.

Up on the table,
Mouse found something
sweet and sparkly...

It was a
cookie.

and something
warm and melty...

It was hot cocoa.

and something
cool and sticky.

It was a candy cane.

Next to the window,
Mouse found something
jingly and glinty...

It was a jingle bell.

and something
bright and flickery...

It
was
a
candle.

and something
fine and silvery.

It was an angel.

High on the mantle,
Mouse found something
soft and felty...

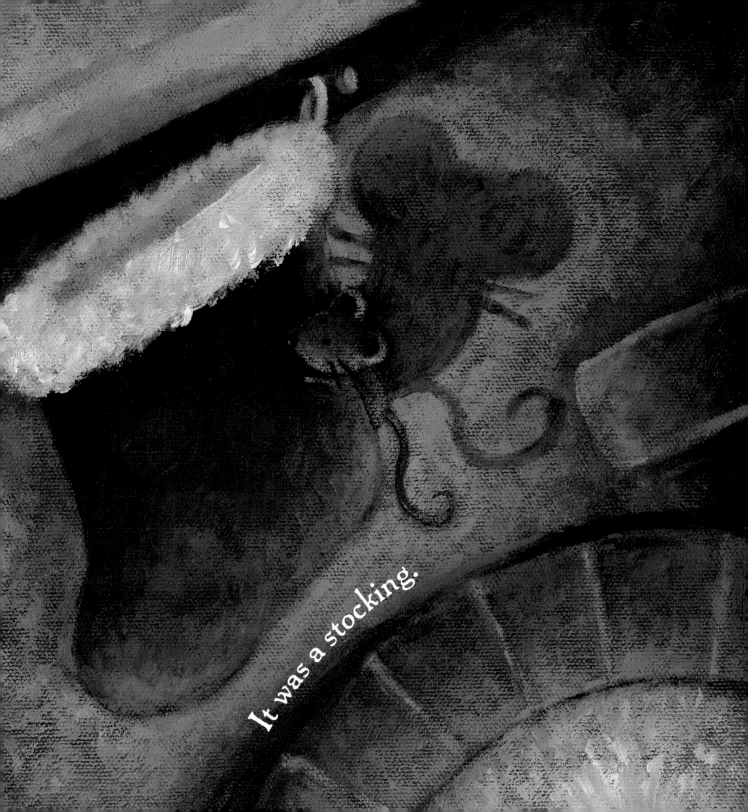

It was a stocking.

and something
white and floaty...

It
was
a
snow
globe.

and something
tinkly and twirly.

It was a music box.

Then there in the corner,
Mouse found something
tall and prickly...

It
was
a
tree.

and something
boxy and ribbony—
lots and lots of them!

Presents!

Then Mouse
found someone
whiskery
and jolly.

It was Santa Claus!

And Santa whispered,
"'Tis your very first Christmas
and all through the house
no one is loved more
than you,...

little mouse."